A Pride of Princesses

Princess Tales from Around the World

collected, retold, and annotated by
SHIRLEY CLIMO

illustrated by
ANGELO TILLERY

HarperTrophy®
A Division of HarperCollinsPublishers

For Sally, of course
—S.C.

To my three princesses
Toniya, Brianna, and Destiny
—A.T.

Harper Trophy® is a registered trademark of HarperCollins Publishers Inc.

A Pride of Princesses
Text copyright © 1996 by Shirley Climo
Illustrations copyright © 1999 by Angelo

Library of Congress Cataloging-in-Publication Data
Climo, Shirley.
  A pride of princesses : princess tales from around the world / collected, retold,
annotated by Shirley Climo ; illustrated by Angelo Tillery.
    p.   cm.
  Summary: Presents retellings of seldom-heard princess tales, featuring such
heroines as White Jade, Gulnara, and Vasilisa the Frog Princess. A discussion of
princess lore precedes each selection.
    ISBN 0-06-442102-3 (pbk.)
    1. Fairy tales.   2. Princesses—Folklore.   [1. Fairy Tales.   2. Folklore.
3. Princesses—Folklore.]   I. Tillery, Angelo, ill.   II. Title.
PZ8.C56Pr   1999   98-41740
398.22—dc21   CIP
                                                                     AC

Typography by Hilary Zarycky
❖
Newly Illustrated Harper Trophy Edition, 1999

Originally published in 1996 as a picture book,
with illustrations by Ruth Sanderson

Visit us on the World Wide Web!
http://www.harperchildrens.com

Contents

Introduction

Once upon a time there was a princess. . . .

Many of our favorite fairy tales begin like that. As soon as you read those words, you realize that you're about to meet someone special.

You already know quite a few European princesses. Thanks to Jacob and Wilhelm Grimm and other storytellers, Cinderella, Snow White, Sleeping Beauty, and Rapunzel are old friends. But around the world are hundreds of princesses that you've not yet met, and hundreds of stories about them that you've not yet heard. Some were simply forgotten over the years. Others were never known beyond the borders of their own countries. The princesses in this book have been waiting, like buried treasure, for someone like you to discover them.

Each chapter in *A Treasury of Princesses* is about a particular princess from a particular place. Although they come from different parts of the world, all of the princesses share something in common. At the story's end, each princess gets what she deserves.

She lives happily ever after.

The Moon Maidens

Thousands of years ago, when Egyptians gazed up at the nighttime sky they thought they saw the face of the man in the moon staring back at them. They said that he'd been banished to the heavens as a punishment for misbehaving on earth.

For a princess, starring in the sky was a reward.

Stargazing people in early Estonia said that the Milky Way was the wedding veil of a sky princess named Lindu. The ancient Greeks also saw royal maidens in the outlines of the stars. One, the constellation called Andromeda, was named for the beautiful Ethiopian princess who was saved from a sea serpent. Pacific people in Samoa and Tonga have maidens-in-the-sky myths, too.

The Ojibway people tell of a chief's daughter who left her family to become a bright star in the nighttime sky. In Japan, "The Shining Princess" tells the opposite story. A star princess leaves her heavenly home to come down to earth.

In a Romanian folktale and a Zuni legend, the caretakers of the sun and the moon are brother and sister. In this old story from China, two royal sisters and their brother share those same roles.

In China, in ancient times, people believed that the world was divided into three kingdoms. The Emperor of the Earth ruled the land. The Emperor of the Seas commanded the waters. And the Emperor of the Heavens watched over the sky. Each ruler tended to his own territory, not bothering the others, so they seldom quarreled.

Of the three, the Emperor of the Heavens was the most powerful. At his command, rain fell, wind whistled, and lightning cracked the clouds. His warriors, dressed in bright armor, were the shining stars, and meteors streaking through the sky were his fiery dragons. The sun itself was home to his son, the Sky Prince. But of all he owned and ordered, the emperor was proudest of his two daughters, the Princesses of the Palace of the Moon.

Although both of these maidens were beautiful, they did not look alike. The princess named White Jade was slender and as pale and delicate as the new moon. The princess known as Golden Bird was plump and as rosy bright as the harvest moon. But what truly delighted their father was the princesses' cleverness with their needles. The two sisters stitched the lacy Milky Way, hung out bands of glimmering moonbeams, and decorated the nighttime sky with their dazzling embroideries.

"My heavenly princesses are without equal in any kingdom," boasted their father the emperor.

Such praise made White Jade blush and Golden Bird cast down her eyes, and they quickly bent over their needlework again.

Those on earth also heard the emperor's brag. Women, from girls to grandmothers, went out to gaze at the heavens and judge the Moon Maidens' work for themselves.

"In the hands of the princesses, even ordinary needles twinkle like stars," they agreed. None of them, young or old, went back to bed. They stayed awake all night, watching White Jade and Golden Bird work on their gleaming embroideries.

Babies, left alone, began to cry, and the mothers hurried to fetch them. But when the babies saw the moon, they howled even louder, for each wanted to hold the shiny ball.

Then boys and men ran outside to find the cause of such commotion. Speechless, they stared at the sky. They ignored the tapestry of tiny jewel-like stitches that stretched high above their heads. Instead they gawked, awestruck, at the lovely princesses themselves.

"In all the universe, these Moon Maidens are the most exquisite," cried a poet. At once he took up brush and ink to write a poem telling everyone in China about the beautiful sewing sisters.

Teachers and students scrambled up the

slippery tiled roofs of their schools to gaze at White Jade and Golden Bird. Farmers left their fields and warriors deserted their posts to scale the mountains for a better look. Nightly, people pushed and elbowed each other to be first to see the moonrise.

The poet, tired from staying up all night, could not write another word. Drowsy students dozed at their desks in the daytime, farmers were too weary to plant the rice, and warriors fell sound asleep with their swords in their hands. Mistakes were made in everything, and nothing at all was done on time.

Even so, the princesses sat and sewed in the moonlight.

The Emperor of the Earth was furious. Shaking the ground with every footstep, he burst in on the Emperor of the Heavens.

"Your Princesses of the Palace of the Moon have turned day and night upside down," the earthly ruler rumbled. "Do something!"

The heavenly emperor did not want to break the peace between land and sky. "A thousand apologies, Honorable Cousin," he said. "Something shall be done."

Clapping his hands, he called for his daughters. When he told them of the earthly emperor's complaint, both maidens nodded. The princesses were modest and knew it was not proper for men to stare at them. Such worldly attention was alarming.

"Perhaps we could pull our embroideries over our heads," White Jade suggested.

"Or conceal ourselves at the back side of the moon," said Golden Bird.

The emperor frowned and tugged on his beard. "A princess does not hide," he declared. "Something must hide you instead."

The emperor ordered the winds of the four directions to blow a curtain of clouds over the face of the moon. The sky was blacker than a cormorant's wing, and those on the land below stumbled about in the darkness. Not even the thinnest ray of light could pierce the thick and woolly veil. Still, the Emperor of the Earth was pleased because, without the Moon Maidens to watch, the people slept by night and worked by day. The Emperor

8

of the Heavens was pleased to have avoided a quarrel. And Princess White Jade and Princess Golden Bird were happy to stitch undisturbed.

But the Emperor of the Seas was most unhappy. Without the stars to guide them, ships were lost. Fish floundered about in panic and the night fishermen tangled their nets. No turtles crawled ashore to lay their eggs. Worst of all, the moon could no longer work its magic on the tides. Sometimes the waves rushed in, swamping the sands, and other times the sea shrank so that only a puddle was left.

Even so, the princesses sat and sewed.

At last, the Emperor of the Seas whirled into the sky on a typhoon and roared, "Give us back the moon!"

The mighty Emperor of the Heavens paled before such anger. "If that is your desire, Noble Cousin," he replied. But his heart despaired.

"What now?" he asked his daughters. "By trying to please everyone, I please no one, least of all myself."

Princess White Jade bowed to her father.

"We have been talking," she said, "Golden Bird and I."

"With your permission," said her sister, "we wish to trade places with our royal brother in the sun."

"What nonsense is this?" cried the emperor.

"The Sky Prince may live in the Palace of the Moon," explained White Jade, "and we can move to the Pagoda of the Sun."

Their father shook his head. "Now men stare at you by moonlight. Surely many more would gape at you in sunlight."

"We have thought of an answer to that," the sisters replied. "Please ask our brother to help us."

The Emperor of the Heavens shrugged. He was certain that the Sky Prince would not consent to such a scheme. But he agreed. "I shall speak to him," he said.

At twilight, that time when the sun has set and the moon has not yet risen, the emperor visited the Pagoda of the Sun. He found his son dozing on the throne, his head in his hands.

"Forgive me, Worthy Father," said the Sky

Prince, jumping up, "but I am sleepy. After waking the sun at dawn, I am too busy to blink until I put it to bed at dusk."

"Would some other life better suit you?" asked the emperor.

"I would willingly trade all this glory," said the Sky Prince, waving his hand at the shining golden pagoda, "for the chance to rest now and then."

For a few moments, the emperor was silent. Then, in a voice that shook the sky like thunder, he proclaimed, "So be it!"

That night, the princesses carefully rolled up their silks and packed a chest with their threads and their dozens and dozens of sharp embroidery needles. Then a dragon chariot carried White Jade and Golden Bird across the ceiling of heaven to the Pagoda of the Sun. Another chariot brought the Sky Prince to the Palace of the Moon.

On earth, people saw two meteors hurtling through the sky. "See that?" they exclaimed. "The dragons are flying tonight!"

Not until the meteors disappeared did they

realize the Moon Maidens had vanished, too. The poet was quite distressed, but many of the girls and young women were pleased to discover a man in the moon instead.

The next morning, the Sun Sisters—for now that is what they were—set to their tasks. The princesses embroidered the sunrise clouds with orange and gold and the sunset clouds with rose and violet. They stitched a many-colored rainbow banner to stretch across the sky after a shower.

No one stared at them as they worked. For those who dared to look up at the sun felt a thousand tiny prickles sting their eyes. Some said that the sunbeams caused their eyes to smart. But others, far wiser, quickly looked away. They knew that what they felt were jabs from White Jade's and Golden Bird's dozens of needles. Even today, anyone foolish enough to look directly at the sun will surely feel the pain of the princesses' displeasure.

Gulnara

To be wise has many meanings.

Sometimes being wise means using your wits. In "The Carrot Counter," a story that's been told in Bohemia for four hundred years, Princess Emma escapes from a wicked magician when she tricks him into counting every carrot in his field twice. "Molly Whuppie," an English heroine, outsmarts a giant three times. As a reward, she marries the king's son. In "Not Driving, Not Riding," a story from Norway, a clever princess earns her royal crown by solving the prince's riddle.

Being wise can also mean being sensible. Common sense helps the princess succeed in the Russian tale "Vasilisa the Wise."

A few centuries ago, a wisewoman was one who studied the stars and knew both charms and cures. Although that kind of wisewoman appears in the next story, it is Princess Gulnara who shows the most wisdom.

"Gulnara" is a tale from *The Arabian Nights*. These stories, more than a thousand years old, were probably first told in India. Legend credits Scheherazade, a Persian queen, with putting the stories together. By telling a different tale every night for one thousand and one nights, Scheherazade entertained the sultan and saved her own life. And that was certainly wise!

In Arabia, a thousand years ago, there was a ruler named Shah Khunoo. The shah was just and treated all his subjects fairly, from the wealthiest silk merchant to the poorest camel boy. To know his people better, Khunoo sometimes disguised himself and wandered unnoticed through crowded city streets. One summer afternoon, when the air was hot and heavy with dust, he stopped at a well to drink. Three sisters were there, talking as they filled their water jugs.

"Last night I dreamed I married the shah's

baker," said the oldest sister, "and I ate all the honeycakes I wanted."

"Oh?" The second sister shrugged. "I dreamed I married the shah's cook and ordered every dish that I desired."

"My dream was the best," the youngest of the three declared. "For in it I married Shah Khunoo himself and had children as bright as the sun."

The sisters giggled at their foolishness, but the shah nodded his turbaned head thought-fully.

Soon after, Shah Khunoo sent for the three sisters. The frightened maidens knelt before his throne, faces to the floor.

"You know me not," said the shah, "yet I know your hearts' desires." He pointed to the oldest sister. "Today you shall have your wish and marry the royal baker.

"Tomorrow you shall wed my cook," he told the second sister.

Then, smiling, he took the youngest sister by her hand. "In two days' time, I shall make you my wife and my queen."

Since the shah's word was the law of the land, all three sisters had their dream weddings. But soon the older girls tired of being married to a mere baker and lowly cook. They envied their sister, a queen in a palace of pink marble, and schemed ways to spoil her happiness.

Before the year was out, the queen bore a son. Her older sisters attended her and snatched the baby before she even saw him. Putting the boy in a basket, they set him adrift in the stream that flowed past the palace.

"The little prince is dead," the sisters told the shah. "He never drew the breath of life."

When he heard this, Shah Khunoo wiped tears from his eyes.

But the prince was far from dead. His lusty cries frightened the fish, scattered the swans, and caught the ear of the shah's gardener. That old man pulled the basket from the brook and hastened home with the baby.

"Praise Allah!" he cried to his wife. "He sent us a son!"

The gardener and his wife named their

newfound baby Bahman and loved him as their own.

The very next year the queen gave birth to another boy and, a few minutes later, to a girl as well. Again, her two sisters attended her. Those wicked women hid these babies in a basket too, and sent it downstream like the first.

"Twins!" the sisters told Shah Khunoo. "But, alas, neither lived. You have lost another prince . . . and a princess, also."

The shah tore his hair and rubbed his face with ashes. In his grief, he accused the queen. "You are to blame for this misery!" he raged. "Be gone from my sight!"

The youngest sister was banished, sent to live in a mud-walled hut scarcely bigger than a dovecote.

As before, the shah's gardener found the basket with the babies. "Allah has blessed us again—and again!" he exclaimed.

The old man and his wife named the second prince Perviz and the princess Gulnara. For more than a dozen years they cared tenderly for the three children. They taught them to write poems and do sums, to play the lute and ride horses. But the old couple could not tell the children where they came from, for that they did not know themselves.

Then, quite suddenly, the gardener and his wife took ill and died. From that day on, the children looked after each other.

One day, while the two princes were hunting pigeons for the cookpot, a wandering wisewoman called on Gulnara.

"Please, child, I need food to eat and a rug to rest on."

"I will gladly share with you, grandmother," said Gulnara.

Gulnara spread her own soft mat on the floor so that the woman could kneel and say her prayers. She picked a melon from the garden and fetched bread from the outdoor oven. The wisewoman ate as if she had not tasted food since the last full moon. When she was done, she put her hand on Gulnara's head.

"In return for your kindness," she said, "I shall tell you of three marvels. The first is a tree whose leaves never fall and which grows lovelier with every season."

Gulnara nodded.

"The second is water that shines like gold. One drop fills a fountain and it never runs dry."

Gulnara smiled.

"The third is a bird with song so sweet that every other bird joins in. And," the old woman whispered, "this songbird can speak words as well."

Gulnara jumped up. "I would like to hear that for myself."

"Follow the camel track that leads to India," the wisewoman directed, and then she disappeared through the low archway.

When her two brothers returned, Gulnara repeated what her visitor had said. "I must find the tree, the golden water, and the wondrous bird!" she exclaimed.

"No, little sister," said Bahman. "Such a quest is not fitting for a girl. I will get them for you."

Gulnara said nothing, and Perviz saddled the

swift-paced stallion for his brother. Before he left, Bahman put his dagger on the table.

"As long as this blade is bright, I am well," he said.

Then Bahman jumped on his horse and galloped down the caravan trail toward India. When he had traveled for sixteen days and nights, he saw a tall mountain looming before him. On its slopes grew a forest of black rocks. At its base sat an ancient hermit thoughtfully wrapping his long beard around his fingers.

"Long life to you, old uncle," said Bahman. "Can you tell me where to find the tree of seasons, the golden water, and the sweet-singing bird?"

"On the crest of yonder mountain," the hermit replied. "But those who climb it do not come down again."

"Warnings do not frighten me."

"Then go." The hermit sighed. "But neither look back at the rocks nor pay mind to their jeers."

Bahman tethered his horse and started on foot up the steep mountain. The path twisted in and out among the black rocks, and a huge boulder broke loose, almost crushing him. As the stone rolled past, it rumbled, "You will be next!"

Forgetting the hermit's words, Bahman spun about and shook his fist. And he became a black rock, too.

At home, the dagger on the table turned a rusty red.

"Bahman is in danger!" cried Perviz. "I must help him."

"Take me with you," begged Gulnara. "Since I told him of the three magical things, I am to blame."

"No, little sister." Perviz patted her arm. "The journey is too dangerous for you." He laid a string of pearls beside the dagger. "As long as this strand is unbroken, I am well."

Then Perviz saddled his stout-hearted mare and trotted down the camel track toward India. He rode for twenty-one days and nights before he came to the mountain of black rocks. He saw Bahman's stallion grazing there, and beside the horse sat the hermit.

The old man gave Perviz the same advice he had given his older brother. But Perviz, even more determined than Bahman, slid off the mare and scrambled up the mountain anyway. He zigzagged between the giant rocks, never looking behind him.

"Mouse-boy!" the black rocks jeered. "Worthless son of a worthless father!"

Perviz ignored their taunts until he heard, "Your brother is a weakling and a coward."

"Liar!" cried Perviz.

That one word turned him to stone.

At home, the string of pearls broke and scattered on the floor. Gulnara knew what she must do.

She filled a sack with dates, climbed on her short-legged pony, and started down the caravan road. For thirty-five days, she jogged through a sea of sand beneath the fiery sun. For thirty-five nights, she shivered beneath the frosty stars. At last the black rocks loomed before her like a crowd of demons.

She left her pony beside the mare and stallion. Like Bahman and Perviz, Gulnara heard the hermit's advice. Unlike her brothers, she let nothing distract her. So as not to forget and turn her head, she wound a scarf about her neck. To muffle any voices, she stopped her ears with wool. To keep from crying out, she stuffed her cheeks with dates. Only then was she ready.

Slowly, Gulnara picked her way up the mountain. Thorns snagged her clothes and a landslide of stones made her stumble. She heard mocking laughter, even through the wool, and voices that grew ever louder until all the rocks seemed to be shouting at once. They scoffed at her brothers and scorned Gulnara, calling, "Shame! Shame!" and "Go home, useless girl!"

She did not answer. She stared straight ahead and put one foot after the other until she reached the top of the mountain.

Once there, Gulnara looked about in disbelief. There was no tree of all seasons, only a leafless branch. There was no golden water, only a dirty puddle. A bird, feathers drooping, huddled in a cage, but its song was no more than a chirp.

"There is no magic here." Tears stung Gulnara's eyes. "Nor are my brothers, either."

She picked up the branch, hung the birdcage on it, filled her cup with the muddy water, and started down the mountain.

The path was slippery, and Gulnara stumbled. Water splashed from the cup onto the black rocks. The stones sizzled and steamed as the drops struck them, and the air swirled with mist. When it cleared, Gulnara saw that a man stood where each stone had been.

She ran from rock to rock, sprinkling magic water everywhere. Two of the bigger boulders became Bahman and Perviz. Soon hundreds of stones, large and small, had human forms again. The grateful men marched after Gulnara as if she were a general.

"Go," she told them. "You are free men again."

Gulnara, Bahman, and Perviz rode home, with Gulnara holding the cup and the branch,

and with the birdcage tied to her saddle.

"What good are a stick, a sick bird, and an empty cup?" asked her brothers.

"We'll see," Gulnara replied.

When they reached their cottage, Gulnara hurried into the garden. She poured the last drop of muddy water into a basin. It spouted up in a fountain, shining like gold in the sunlight.

She planted the branch in the ground. The next morning, it was bursting with blossoms. She hung the birdcage from a limb. The bird fluffed its feathers and began to trill so lovely a melody that songbirds, from larks to the smallest sparrows, joined in.

Word of this marvelous garden spread throughout the countryside. Shah Khunoo, dressed as a beggerman, came to see for himself. The three children welcomed the shabby stranger.

"What a splendid tree!" he exclaimed. "Even the shah has nothing so fine!"

When he heard the bird, he told them, "Not even the shah has such a sweet-voiced songbird!"

He tasted the water from the golden fountain and declared, "No nectar is so refreshing." He gazed at Bahman, Perviz, and Gulnara and added, "The shah was never so fortunate as to have children like you."

At that the bird stopped singing and chirruped, "He has, if he will but believe his eyes."

Amazed, they stared at the bird. The shah found his voice first. "I understand your words but not your meaning."

The bird explained how the queen's sisters stole the babies and how the gardener found them. "That's what I saw from the palace roof," it said. "Now you can see for yourself."

The shah blinked. All three children were as bright as the sun, and Gulnara was the image of her mother the queen. "I am Shah Khunoo, your father," he said, pulling the tattered hood from his head. "I ask your forgiveness."

The brothers bowed and nodded their heads, but Gulnara answered wisely, "You must seek pardon from the queen first."

On seeing Bahman, Perviz, and Gulnara, the queen was too full of joy to have room for anger. All of them lived happily in the pink marble palace, except for the queen's sisters. Those two dared not show their faces anywhere in Arabia again.

Prince Ivan and the Frog Princess

⬥━●━◆━●━⬥

In most fairy tales, a princess is enchanting. In some, she is also enchanted. Because their mothers ate forbidden foods, Rapunzel, a German princess, and Tangletop, a Norwegian princess, were born under spells.

In France, Sleeping Beauty got the gift of a one-hundred-year nap because a spiteful fairy wasn't invited to her christening. In a different French tale, another uninvited fairy vows that Princess Mayblossom will be "the unluckiest of the unlucky."

At any age, in any place, a princess may fall under a spell. If she's changed into something else, she must remain in that form until someone breaks her enchantment.

A sad Irish legend tells how Princess Etain became a butterfly. Margaret, daughter of the King of Northumberland, is turned into a monstrous dragon in an English fairy tale. In an old Italian tale, the princess becomes an enchanted fish.

Princesses in swan feathers are found in Germany, Africa, and Hungary. A story from Bulgaria tells about a princess who is turned into a dove, and in the Andes Mountains of Colombia, Princess Quira appears as a golden duck swimming on a lake.

Sometimes a prince or princess is bewitched as a frog. According to an Alaskan story, that's what happened to the daughter of a Tlingit chief. In this *skazka*, a fairy tale from Russia, the tsar's son takes an ugly frog as his princess bride.

In old Russia, across the blue salt sea, beyond the green forest, behind the gray granite mountains, lay the kingdom of Tsar Verlioka. This tsar, a wise old ruler, was the father of three handsome sons.

When the time came for the three princes

to marry, Tsar Verlioka told them, "Each of you will shoot an arrow in the air. Whoever claims the arrow, wherever it falls, will be your bride."

Peter, the oldest son, took aim first. His golden arrow whistled over the mountains, arched above the treetops, and then plunged toward the sea. It fell on the deck of a fine merchant ship, at the feet of the captain's lovely daughter.

Marko, the second son, shot his silver arrow next. It skimmed over the mountains and dropped to earth in the forest. The daughter of a *boyar*, a nobleman, discovered it there.

Ivan, the youngest son, was last to take his turn. Although he pulled his bowstring almost to breaking, his brass arrow did not fly far or high. It struck the rocky mountainside and splashed into the swamp below.

Ivan waded into the muddy water in search of it. Any noise, even the whine of a gnat, startled him, for he'd heard that the witch Baba-Yaga sometimes lurked in the bog. Ivan did not want to cross her path, for she was as likely to eat a man as greet him. As he peered around him, he stumbled over a very large and ugly frog. Clutched in its webbed toes was Ivan's brass arrow.

"Give me my arrow!" Ivan ordered. Then he added, "Please."

The frog did not move. It did not even twitch. It fixed its bulging eyes on Ivan and croaked, *"Kva! Kva!"*

"Stubborn creature!" Ivan cried. "The soup kettle is where you belong!" He grasped both frog and arrow, thrust them into his knapsack, and trudged home.

Ivan's brothers were waiting at the palace. Peter stood beside the captain's lovely daughter. Marko held the noble lady's hand. Tsar Verlioka asked Ivan, "Who found your arrow, my son?"

"Look!" Ivan upended his knapsack, spilling out the frog.

"Ugh!" cried the captain's daughter and the noble lady.

"What shall I do now?" Ivan asked his father.

"Do?" The tsar tugged his chin whiskers. "Why, you must marry the frog, of course. That is your fate."

Ivan stared at his father, horrified, but the frog grinned, stretching its mouth wide.

The three princes shared one wedding celebration. Peter's bride, whose name was Sonya, rode to the church in a golden carriage. Olga, Marko's wife-to-be, arrived in a coach of silver. Ivan called his frog Vasilisa and carried her to the ceremony in an old brass samovar used for making tea.

Vasilisa did not like being caged in a teapot. *"Nyet! Nyet!"* she complained, bumping against the lid until Ivan let her out. From then on, she traveled on his shoulder. Nor would she eat flies like other frogs. Instead, she squatted on the supper table and flicked her long tongue into Ivan's soup. At bedtime, she plopped down on the pillow beside his head.

After a month had passed, Tsar Verlioka called his sons to him. "I would measure the talents of your wives," said the tsar. He gave each prince a length of fine linen. "Tonight, bid your wife to stitch this into a shirt."

When Peter gave his cloth to Princess Sonya, she cut one shirtsleeve too short and the other too long. The seams she sewed were as wavy as rivers.

When Marko gave his cloth to Princess Olga, she poked her finger with the needle and began to cry.

Ivan took his cloth to the Frog Princess and told her, "My father would have you make this into a shirt."

"Tak?" croaked Vasilisa. "So?" She hopped up and down on the linen and tore it to shreds with her toes.

"You—you are nothing but a senseless ANIMAL!" Ivan shouted. He ran out, slamming the door behind him.

The frog dragged the tatters of cloth across the floor and threw them out the window. Then she turned a backward somersault and croaked, *"Kva!"* A shirt, perfect to the last button, flapped into the room and dropped at her feet.

The next morning, the three brothers took their three shirts to their father. Tsar Verlioka scorned Princess Sonya's lopsided sewing. He scowled at the speckles of blood on Princess Olga's efforts. Then he held up Vasilisa's shirt.

"Marvelous!" the tsar exclaimed, and put it on at once.

Ivan smiled at his Frog Princess.

One month later, Tsar Verlioka said to his sons, "I would know which princess is best at baking. Tell each to make a loaf of bread for my breakfast."

When Sonya heard that, she grumbled to Olga, "Another test! Another chance for Vasilisa to show off."

"Or practice witchcraft," warned Olga. "Let's watch. We will see for ourselves what that hideous frog is up to."

The two squeezed inside a kitchen cupboard, leaving the door open a crack to spy on their sister-in-law. They giggled when Vasilisa flopped clumsily onto the table, but she pretended not to hear. First, the frog jumped into the bin of flour, scattering it like snow around the room. Next, she spilled a bucket of dish-water and broke a dozen eggs on the floor. With a broom, she swept everything into a pan and pushed the pan into the oven. "Bake! Bake! Bake!" she chanted in her hoarse voice.

Soon the kitchen smelled deliciously of fresh-baked bread. Vasilisa left the crusty loaf to cool and hopped out the door.

Sonya and Olga crept from the cupboard. Since they dared not steal Vasilisa's loaf, they mixed a batch of sticky dough, exactly as the Frog Princess had. Then they shoved it into pans and put them in the oven, and com-manded, "Hurry up, bread. Bake!"

Smoke poured from the stove and swirled overhead like thunderclouds. Sonya snatched the bread from the oven, but the loaves were already as black as cinders and as hard as bricks.

At breakfast the next morning, Prince Ivan was gleeful when Tsar Verlioka left no doubt whose bread he liked the best.

◆ ◆ ◆

A third month passed, and this time the tsar told his sons, "We shall have a ball and invite everyone to meet your wives."

On the day of the dance, Sonya and Olga put on their prettiest gowns and their brightest jewels. Vasilisa wore her drab green skin as always and hid inside the brass samovar.

"Come out!" Ivan ordered. "I must present you."

The lid on the samovar jiggled and a loud *"Nyet!"* came from beneath it. Ivan had to go without his Frog Princess.

The great hall of the palace swarmed with *boyars* and their ladies, with rich merchants and their wives, with soldiers and scholars, with shopkeepers and blacksmiths, with farmers and their families. They cheered when they caught sight of Princess Sonya and Princess Olga. But when Ivan appeared without Princess Vasilisa, rumors buzzed about the ballroom like mosquitoes.

"I hear she's a toad," said a gossip, "or something worse."

All of a sudden, a gust of wind blew open

the doors and in swept an enchanting maiden. Her hair was the color of autumn wheat and her cheeks were as rosy as summer apples. Her dress, as white as winter snow, was scattered with pearls.

Tsar Verlioka bowed and said, "Please join us, my lady."

"Do you not know me, dear father?" she replied. "I am Vasilisa, Ivan's own Frog Princess."

The tsar stared at her, open-mouthed. When he found his voice again, he said, "Then, daughter, honor me with a dance."

The musicians played tune after tune as Tsar Verlioka and Princess Vasilisa whirled around the ballroom. All the crowd applauded except for Peter, Marko, and their wives. Sonya and Olga were too jealous, and the princes too confused.

"Is she truly your wife?" they asked Ivan. "What happened?"

"I do not know. But I am going to find out."

Prince Ivan hurried to Vasilisa's room to look inside the samovar. In his haste, he

slipped on something soft but bumpy. Ivan bent down. At his feet lay the warty green skin of a frog.

"The little coat of my Frog Princess!" He waved it like a banner. "Without it, Vasilisa can never again be a frog!"

Ivan dashed down the stairs and threw the frog skin into the kitchen stove. The skin hissed and crackled on the coals and crumpled to ashes, leaving behind a telltale wisp of smoke.

Princess Vasilisa found Ivan in the kitchen. "Why did you leave . . . ?" She stopped and sniffed. "Is something burning?"

"Your awful frog skin!" cried Ivan. "Good riddance to it!"

"You have ruined everything!" Tears splashed Vasilisa's cheeks. "Kostchey the Sorcerer changed me into a frog. A frog I had to stay unless someone took me as his wife for three times thirty days. My time was up at midnight. But you . . ." She dabbed at her eyes. ". . . You burned my frog skin an hour too soon!"

"Forgive me." Ivan dropped to his knees. "Tell me what I must do."

"Seek me in the thirtieth kingdom, at the house of the witch Baba-Yaga."

Vasilisa clapped her hands. Her gown became a cloak of white feathers and the pearls became drops of dew. As Ivan watched, Vasilisa turned into a swan and flew out the window.

Prince Ivan bid farewell to his family and set out to find his Frog Princess. He climbed over the gray granite mountains, tramped through the green forest, and sailed across the blue salt sea. He traveled for weeks and months and even years, wearing out four horses and six pairs of boots. At the far border of the thirtieth kingdom, Ivan came to a little hut balanced on two spindly chicken legs. He guessed at once who lived there.

Bravely, Ivan marched to the door. Boldly, he lifted the latch and walked in. Asleep before the fireplace was an old lady, bony as a skeleton, with knees like bed knobs and elbows as sharp as spades. Her long nose was poked up the chimney and she was snoring and snuffling as loudly as a pig.

"Baba-Yaga," Ivan whispered.

The witch sat up and screeched, "I smell a Russian!"

"I am Ivan Tsarevitch, Baba-Yaga."

"Ah!" She pinched his arm. "Just in time for my supper."

"I . . . I cannot stay. I am searching for my wife, Vasilisa."

"Your frog wife works for Kostchey the Sorcerer," said Baba-Yaga, scowling. "But she stops here every morning."

"Then I shall see her!" Ivan exclaimed.

"Swamp creatures. That's what you will see." Baba-Yaga bobbed her head.

"Catch them. Hold them.
Do not let them free.
Should you grasp an arrow,
Snap it on your knee!"

"I don't understand . . ." Ivan began, but the witch had fallen asleep again, this time with her feet stuck up the chimney.

42

While Ivan was wondering what to do next, he heard wings flapping and a white swan swooped through the door.

"Vasilisa!" he shouted, catching the bird in his arms. The swan struggled, shedding her feathers, and became a frog.

"I know you now!" said Ivan, holding on tight. The frog's lumpy skin became scales and a mud fish flopped in his hands.

"Please!" cried Ivan. "Hold still!" The slippery scales of the fish became the soft fur of a weasel.

The weasel snarled and snapped at Ivan. "Do not bite, dear wife," he begged. Wiggling, the weasel turned into a swamp snake.

The snake coiled and hissed, but Ivan did not loosen his grip. Then suddenly it became as stiff and straight as a poker.

"My brass arrow!" Ivan exclaimed, for that's what it was.

Remembering Baba-Yaga's words, he squeezed his eyes shut and struck the arrow sharply on his knee. The arrow snapped with a crack like thunder. Ivan opened his eyes and found himself clasping the hands of Princess Vasilisa.

"Now you have truly broken Kostchey's spell." Vasilisa smiled at him. "Ivan, my husband, let us go home."

The return journey took no time at all, for Baba-Yaga sped them through the sky in her flying mortar, pushing the clouds aside with her broom.

When they reached the tsar's palace, Vasilisa said to her, "Thank you, little mother, for helping us."

"Thank YOU!" The witch chuckled. "I enjoyed playing a trick on that villain, Kostchey."

The whole kingdom celebrated the return of the prince and princess. In time, Ivan sat on the throne as tsar, and Vasilisa sat beside him as tsarina.

Two Brides for Five Heads

Strength and bravery are most often the trade-marks of a prince. But a princess can be called upon to show great courage, too.

"Hinemoa and Tutanekai" is a Maori tale from New Zealand. Princess Hinemoa defies her father and swims across Lake Rotarua in the dark of night to join Tutanekai, the boy she loves.

The maiden in a Japanese tale dives down to the underwater cave of the Dragon King and recovers a sacred pearl for her prince. In long-ago China, the girl Li Chi won the love of the emperor by slaying a terrifying serpent.

Legend tells how Pocahontas, daughter of the Algonquin Chief Powhatan, risked her own neck to save that of the Englishman John Smith. In "Rushycoat and the King's Son," a Cinderella story from Kentucky, Rushycoat weds the king's son, but only after she has put to flight a herd of wild horses, a band of wild hogs, and a dozen angry bears.

"Two Brides for Five Heads" is a Xhosa story from South Africa. Daily life was dangerous for the Xhosa people, and both men and women needed courage. The strength of a woman's arms was more important than the beauty of her face.

Xhosa tales are full of magic and were told in the evening, when belief in the supernatural was the strongest. Often one storyteller began, and then others added ideas of their own. Few stories were ever told the same way twice.

In the South Africa of long ago, on the coast of the Indian Ocean near the Great Kei River, there once lived a farmer and his two daughters. The older girl was named Mpunzikazi; the younger was called Mpunzanyana. Both girls were strong and able. Both could run as fast as a bushbuck, and either could aim a throwing stick as well as any boy. Working together, they could thatch the roof of their hut and smear floors and walls with fresh mud, finishing both jobs before sundown.

Many young men in their village wished to marry one or the other of the sisters, but their father refused them all.

"Foolish fellows!" he scoffed. "Do you hope to exchange a few ordinary cows for my extraordinary daughters? Each is worth ten of your choicest cattle."

Not a man among them could pay such a price, so the father went upriver to a larger *kraal*, or village, where the headman was very rich. There he boasted to everyone about his daughters. The chief listened thoughtfully, for he had long sought a bride for his son. No girl had been found who pleased both the boy and his family.

"If what you say is so," said the headman, "and if one of your daughters proves suitable, I will give you fifteen head of cattle and two white goats for her."

"Ho!" gasped the father. He had never

dared to dream of such a large *lobolo*, or bride-payment. But because he loved his daughters, he said, "First I must find out which, if either, girl is willing."

He hurried home, anxious to tell the girls of their good fortune. Mpunzanyana, the younger, was doubtful, but Mpunzikazi, the older, was delighted.

"Of course I shall marry the chief's son! He will give me necklaces and bracelets and red blankets, and I shall eat chicken morning and night."

Soon fifteen head of cattle were tramping about the muddy byre while two fine white goats bleated in the pen. Then Mpunzikazi was eager to go. She refused to delay, not even long enough to change her short skirt for the long one of a married woman. "It would twist about my ankles when I run," she said.

Mpunzikazi would not take anything with her, not even her sleeping mat. "I will have a new one soon enough," she said.

"I will travel with you," offered her father, "and protect you from wild beasts."

"No need," scoffed Mpunzikazi. "Nothing in the world frightens me."

Empty-handed and all alone, Mpunzikazi started up the track toward the rich chief's village. She'd scarcely gone a mile when a jackal crept out of a thicket.

"Let me go first," it suggested, "and show you the way."

"Sly thing! You'll not trick me!" Mpunzikazi clapped her hands. "Go! *Hamba!*"

The jackal bounded away and Mpunzikazi walked on. She walked until she reached the banks of the Kei River. There she sat on a log and rested her tired legs and cooled her burning feet in the water. A frog jumped up beside her.

"Greet–greet–greetings!" it croaked. "Shall I show you the way?"

"Ugly thing! Don't speak to me!" Mpunzikazi retorted. "Soon I shall be a princess."

She shook a stick at the frog, and it splashed into the water. Then Mpunzikazi walked on, trying to catch her shadow that stretched long and thin before her. In the distance, she saw many round huts, with thatched roofs like big straw hats. One towered above the rest, and Mpunzikazi knew it must belong to the rich chief.

An old woman hailed her from the riverbank where she was washing clothes on the rocks. "Where are you going, my daughter?"

"I'm no daughter to an old crone like you!" Mpunzikazi tossed her head and turned her back. "I am going to be the wife of the headman's son."

"Wait!" the woman said. "I shall come, too, and give you some advice if you will listen."

But Mpunzikazi did not wait and she did not listen. Boldly, she marched into the village. She ignored the people's stares and shrugged off their questions, saying only, "I have come to marry the son of the chief."

"He is called Makanda Mahlanu," the old woman mumbled in Mpunzikazi's ear, for she had been hurrying at the girl's heels, "and yonder is his home. When the chief's son returns, his stomach will be empty and growling with hunger. You must have his food ready for him."

With a shrug, Mpunzikazi followed her into the hut. Although the room was large, there was only one small window. The old woman covered it with a blanket.

"To keep out any witches," she whispered.

If there's a witch about, it's likely you, thought Mpunzikazi, but she did not speak aloud.

The woman handed her a sack. "Corn," she said. "You must grind it into flour for mealie cakes." Then the woman knelt down on the dirt floor to watch.

The hut was as dark as a cave. The only light came from the small fire that glowed beneath a kettle in the middle of the room. Mpunzikazi scowled at the old woman, picked up a grinding stone, and began to pound the corn. This was not the welcome she'd expected. "Not . . . at . . . all!" she muttered as she pounded. "I . . . OW!"

Mpunzikazi threw down the grinding stone and popped her hurt thumb in her mouth. "That's enough!" she declared.

She mixed a little water with the lumpy grain, rolled the mixture into cakes, and dropped them in the kettle to boil. "A hungry man will eat anything at all," said Mpunzikazi.

Ignoring the old woman, she lay down beside the fire. Soon she was fast asleep, dreaming of chicken and yams.

A terrible commotion woke Mpunzikazi. The wind howled louder than a pack of hyenas, tearing at the hut and almost toppling the roof pole. Blows shook the door, and a voice bellowed, "Let me in!"

Mpunzikazi caught her breath. What if it was a witch, an *Igqwira*, riding a baboon? "Who . . . is . . . there?" she asked.

"Makanda Mahlanu!"

Slowly, Mpunzikazi got up. Slowly, she opened the door. She screamed.

A huge and hideous snake slithered through the doorway. It had to coil its long tail to squeeze inside, and sharp scales covered its body. Ten bulging eyes, as red as the fire coals, glared at her. The serpent had five heads!

"Makanda Mahlanu," whispered Mpunzikazi,

"Five Heads." That was what the name meant.

"Feed me, girl." Five jaws dropped open, as wide as a crocodile's, and five tongues forked out of five mouths.

"Wulululu!" wailed Mpunzikazi. For the first time in her life, she was terrified. Perhaps this monster meant to eat her! Snatching the kettle with the mealie cakes, she flung it at the snake. "Feed yourself," she cried.

The water had boiled away and the mealies were burned and hard as cinders. As the hot cakes struck, the snake hissed and thrashed its body from side to side. In a fury, its tail whipped Mpunzikazi and she fell to the floor, senseless. Makanda Mahlanu looked at her scornfully and wriggled out the door again.

The old woman carried Mpunzikazi to a nearby hut.

"Your first daughter did not please the son of the chief." That was the message Mpunzikazi's father received.

"Poor Mpunzikazi! We know nothing of her fate," he moaned. "And now we must give back the cows and the two white goats."

"I will go to the rich chief's *kraal*. Perhaps I can please his son and find my sister," said his second daughter.

Although her father feared for her safety, Mpunzanyana would not change her mind. But she did not leave at once.

First she clipped her hair short. She buried the locks in the muddy byre where no witch could find them and cast a spell on her. Then she wound a turban about her head, wrapping it so low on her brow that it almost covered her eyes. Not gazing directly at the chief would show her respect.

Next she put on a long skirt made of new material and stitched with rows of braid. She hung necklaces of colored beads about her neck and slipped shiny brass bands on her arms.

Last, Mpunzanyana rolled her sleeping mat and tucked bread inside for her journey. She put the bundle on her head and started up the same path as her sister.

When Mpunzanyana had gone a little way,

she met a mouse perched on top of an ant-hill.

"Stop!" it squealed. "Do not walk by the river!"

"Will you show me another way?" asked Mpunzanyana.

The mouse ran up a different path, away from the riverbank, and Mpunzanyana followed. Suddenly clouds darkened the sky, thunder rumbled, and rain poured down as if spilling from a thousand water jugs. She was grateful to the mouse, for the river would surely rise and flood.

Mpunzanyana found shelter from the storm beneath a thorn tree and looked about to thank the mouse. But it was not the mouse she saw. What she saw instead made her gasp. "Oh!" Mpunzanyana clapped her hands over her mouth.

Behind her, standing on one leg, was a giant crane. The bird was taller than a man, with white feathers and a red beak. This was no ordinary crane. Thunder crashed when it beat its wings, and when it spit, lightning flashed.

Mpunzanyana shivered. This was the Storm-Maker—the Lightning Bird!

"I—I wish you good day," Mpunzanyana murmured. She took the bread from her bundle and held it out to the crane.

The bird stepped closer and stared at her with eyes as dark as holes. Then it opened its beak, snapped up the bread, and swallowed it whole. Bobbing its head to Mpunzanyana, the crane rasped, "Ahead is the *kraal* of the chief. Whatever happens, do not be afraid."

The Lightning Bird stretched its legs, unfolded its wings, and flew away. At once the rain stopped falling and the sky cleared. Balancing her bundle on top of her head again, Mpunzanyana went on.

As she neared the chief's village, she saw an old woman at the river's edge, trying to fill her jug with the rushing water.

"Where are you going?" the woman asked.

"This is the end of my journey," Mpunzanyana replied. "I have come to meet the chief's son."

"Will you be frightened when you see him?"

"I shall not show fear," Mpunzanyana declared.

"That is good," said the woman, nodding. "Come with me. In the evening, Makanda Mahlanu will return. You must prepare for him."

The old woman led her to the chief's large hut. There she smeared Mpunzanyana's face and neck with red clay paste. "When Makanda Mahlanu arrives, you must be decorated as a bride."

The old woman gave her corn to grind. "When Makanda Mahlanu arrives, he will be very hungry," she said. "You must make mealies for the chief's son."

The old woman sat in the shadows, silently watching, with her chin on her knees.

So that she would not be afraid, Mpunzanyana began to sing softly to herself as she pounded the corn. She sang song after song until every kernel was ground to fine powder. She mixed it with water and patted it into five smooth mealie cakes. When they were cooked, she scooped them from the kettle with a broad stick.

Then she turned to the old woman and said, "If you will, now I shall rest."

Mpunzanyana had scarcely closed her eyes when a violent wind arose. It whistled through the smoke hole, putting out the fire, and ripped the blanket from the window. The door burst open and the snake with five heads rushed in, hissing at Mpunzanyana, raising the windstorm with its whistling breath.

Remembering the words of the Lightning Bird, Mpunzanyana told herself, "I must be brave."

Without blinking, she gazed at Makanda Mahlanu from beneath her turban and said, "With so many mouths, you must be very hungry, Five Heads." Mpunzanyana picked up the five tender cakes and put one in each gaping mouth.

The snake gulped the cakes. "Ha-a-a-ah!" It swayed back and forth, grunting in satisfaction, and the whole hut shook.

Suddenly, something wriggled across Mpunzanyana's bare toes. She gasped and, trembling, lowered her eyes. At her feet lay the

scaly skin of a snake. When she dared to look up, it was into the face of a young man. He wore a collar of beads and blue crane feathers like a Xhosa warrior.

"I am the chief's son," he said. "I took the shape of a snake so I might test the worthiness of one who would be my bride." He smiled at her. "You have courage. That is pleasing to me."

"You please me also, Makanda Mahlanu," answered Mpunzanyana.

"Ah-hah!" chortled the old woman from the shadows. As Five Heads's mother, she was most pleased of all. Surely this maiden deserved to marry the son of a chief.

Mpunzanyana and Makanda Mahlanu were wed. Mpunzikazi, more humble and much wiser, returned home to tend the fifteen head of cattle and milk the two white goats.

After a few years, Makanda Mahlanu became the village headman. He gave Mpunzanyana many ornaments to wear, and honored her as long as she lived.

King Thrushbeard

Being pretty doesn't make a princess pleasing. Nor will being royal turn a wrong to a right. It's hard to find a perfect princess, even in a storybook.

It's easier to sympathize with an imperfect princess. If she makes mistakes or misbehaves, if she's impatient or jealous or sulks about something, then she's acting like the rest of us.

An imperfect princess might tell a fib, like the one in the Scandinavian story "The Three Aunts." She might have tantrums, like the king's daughter in the Scottish "The Princess Who Wanted the Stars." Her curiosity might cause trouble, as it did for the three princesses who opened the forbidden door in the Romanian "The Enchanted Pig." Maybe she never laughs, like the Filipina princess in "Bristlepate," or the German princess in "The Golden Goose."

Perhaps she is simply spoiled. That was the trouble with the princess in the Grimms' "King

Thrushbeard." Variations of this fairy tale are told across Europe, from the icy fjords of Norway to the sunny beaches of Portugal. Since the princess in "King Thrushbeard" was not named, this retelling borrows the name "Lina" from a different story by the brothers Grimm.

Once there was a king who had a beautiful daughter named Lina. Because the queen was dead, the king was both father and mother to Lina. He loved his daughter dearly and treasured her more than gold.

Whatever Princess Lina wanted, she got. Other children were content with hobby horses, but she had a pet pony. Other children rode in wooden carts; Lina traveled in a gilded coach. She did as she pleased, ate what she liked, and never said *"Danke."* Saying "thank you" was a bother.

Princess Lina was as spoiled as she was beautiful.

♦ ♦ ♦

When the princess was sixteen, the king decided it was time she married. Lina agreed, but only if she found someone she fancied. She ordered her many suitors to line up before the throne so that she might inspect them one by one.

"Barrel of butter!" said she of a rather chubby prince.

"Legs like a stork!" she declared of a tall, thin count.

She mocked the younger men, calling them *"Kinder"*—babies—and told older men that they were "as wrinkled as prunes."

She turned up her pretty nose at tsars and earls and found fault with the dukes and lords. She dismissed dozens of brave knights with a scornful wave of her hand. At last only a bearded young king from a nearby country remained. When Princess Lina saw him, she burst out laughing.

"Such bushy whiskers! Take care a bird does not nest in them." She raised her arm. "I dub you King Thrushbeard!"

The young king wheeled about and stamped from the palace.

"Now you have insulted everyone!" moaned her father. "You have made enemies of friends."

Princess Lina shrugged. "Who cares?"

"*I* care!" shouted her father. "And so shall you. Rich or poor, old or young, the first man who sets foot in this palace tomorrow is the one you shall marry!"

"I shan't," screamed the princess. She threw her crown on the floor and ran up the staircase to the tower.

No one came to comfort her. This time Lina did not get her way. Someone else, listening outside the window, vowed to have things his way instead.

When Princess Lina marched into the throne room the next morning, there was a stranger standing just inside the door. He was tall, with clean-shaven cheeks. She might have found him handsome if his shirt had not been so tattered and his trousers torn. Lina scowled at him.

The man smiled back. "You need cheering, Your Highness," he said. "I know how to cure you."

Lifting his battered fiddle, he began to play a jolly tune and sing some silly words. When he finished, he bowed to the king, took off his dirty cap, and held it out for a coin.

"You have earned a rich reward, my good minstrel." The king's voice trembled. "You shall have my daughter as a wife."

The ragged fellow squinted at Lina. "She does not look strong . . . I doubt that she will be very useful . . . but so be it. Beggars cannot be choosers."

"Father, you wouldn't!" the princess cried. "You couldn't!"

The king groaned. "I cannot break my word."

And so Lina had to marry the wandering minstrel. As soon as they were wed, he took the princess by the hand and announced, "Now we'll be off."

"Where is the carriage?" she asked, looking about. "Where is the horse?"

Her husband tapped his boot. "Together we have four good feet. They'll take us where we need to go."

He started down the road, pulling the sulky princess behind him. When they had walked for half a day, they reached a large wood.

"Ah!" said Lina. "Who is the lord of this forest so fine?"

"It belongs to King Thrushbeard,
   And now would be thine,
   If you were his queen," sang the musician.

The princess bit her lip and did not answer. That afternoon, they came to green fields dotted with golden daisies.

Lina asked, "Who is the lord of these meadows so fine?"

"They belong to King Thrushbeard,
   And now would be thine,
   If you were his queen," the musician sang.

"How hateful! Stop singing!" ordered the princess.

They trudged on until they reached a high

hill. At the top, a castle gleamed like a golden crown in the setting sun. Hidden in the shadows below was a tumbledown cottage.

"Who owns this hut, fit only for swine?"

"I do," said the minstrel, "and now it is thine."

Princess Lina pushed open the creaky door. Mice scurried into the corners and spiderwebs brushed against her face. In the dim light from windows dark with dust, she saw a rickety spinning wheel on the hearth and a three-legged stool squatting beside it. The musician pointed to a jumble of straw in one corner and said, "There is your bed, wife."

"A haystack!" she protested. "And call me 'Your Highness.' "

"Your highness of what?" asked the musician. "That was yesterday. Today's today. And you may call me 'husband.' "

"I won't call you at all," said Lina. She sat down on the stool, removed her shoes, and rubbed the blisters on her heels.

"Get up. There's the fire to kindle and supper to make."

"I've never learned to strike a spark and I cannot cook."

"I made a bad bargain when I took you as wife," grumbled the minstrel, lighting the fire. "Now you must earn your keep like any other." He poked in the cupboards, found a measure of oats, and stirred up a pot of porridge.

"Ugh!" said Princess Lina, and turned her bowl upside down.

"Oh? Then you will have nothing to eat," he replied, and scraped the pot clean by himself.

The next day and the days that followed were even worse for the princess. She could not boil an egg without burning it. Whenever she sat down at the spinning wheel, she poked her finger on the spindle. The minstrel bid her try her hand at basket weaving, but Lina's lopsided baskets looked like hats for scarecrows.

Next she sold clay pots, displaying them beside the road in a nearby town. Folks liked to buy from such a pretty lass, and all went well until a horseman galloped past, scattering her wares and breaking them to bits.

"Enough's enough," the minstrel declared. "Go up to the castle. The cook needs a kitchen maid, and you can bring back leftovers from the king's table."

"What king is that?" asked Lina.

"Why, King Thrushbeard, of course."

The musician began to play a merry jig on his fiddle, but Princess Lina was wailing too loudly to hear.

Every day Lina put on an apron and climbed the hill to the castle. There she washed the plates, polished the glasses, and scoured the pots and pans. Each evening she returned to the cottage with her apron pockets stuffed with scraps to divide between her husband and herself. The minstrel smiled when he saw her scattering crumbs for the mice as well. "They are hungry, too," she said.

One morning the cook announced, "Today you must work especially hard. King Thrushbeard is having a wedding feast."

70

Lina dropped a spoon. "Who has he married?"

"Some lucky lass," said the cook. "No one knows her name."

The princess sighed and said, "The luck might have been mine, had I not scorned the love of the king."

The cook paid no attention, for she was busy preparing a hundred different dishes for a thousand wedding guests. Platters were piled high with roasted venison and hare, and ringed with garlands of fat sausages. Huge bowls brimmed with red cabbage and applesauce. The wedding cake was baked in the shape of the castle, and its roof was tiled with sugared almonds.

One by one, Lina carried the dishes into the huge hall. She kept her head down, looking at no one and hoping that none would guess she was a once-proud princess. At last, only the cake remained to be served. Lina parted the velvet curtains to the hall, holding the cake high to hide her face. She did not see the bellpull and caught the toe of her shoe in the tassel.

Lina tripped, the cake fell, and almonds flew everywhere.

"Oh, dear!" she cried. "Poor cook! The king will scold her for hiring me. Poor husband! The cook will blame him for sending me!" Lina buried her face in her hands. "He will say I am hopeless—and he will be right!"

"Wrong!" answered a voice. "At last you are cured of your troubles."

Lina peeped through her fingers and saw the ermine-trimmed hem of the king's robe. But when she glanced up, she saw the familiar face of the minstrel. She jumped to her feet, bewildered. "Who . . . ?"

"I am indeed the king," he said. "I only played the part of minstrel until you showed true concern for others."

"But this feast . . ."

"It is to celebrate our wedding." The king swept his arm around the hall and said, "Now all this is thine."

He led the princess, still in her apron, to the head of the table. "Long live the queen!" the king proclaimed.

Lina smiled and waved, for she saw her father's face among the guests. Speaking loudly so that none would mistake her, she said, "I will be queen only to King Thrushbeard. I beg you, Husband, grow your wonderful whiskers again!"

That is how Princess Lina became Queen Lina. As for King Thrushbeard, if he had another name, no one ever heard it.

The Princess and
the Music-Maker

In stories, a princess is often a prisoner. Sometimes an evil person locks her up for revenge. Sometimes the princess's own parents shut her up for safekeeping.

A German tale, "The Princess Who Was Hidden Underground," tells of a princess kept for years and years in a dark dungeon. In "Glass Mountain," a tale told in southern Europe, a king's daughter waits in a castle at the top of a crystal hill. Any suitor trying to reach her slips and slides down glassy slopes.

Towers are favored as lockups for princesses. Usually a prince comes to the rescue, as in "Rapunzel," but help can come from unexpected sources, too. In the Jewish folktale "The Princess in the Tower," King Solomon shuts away his beautiful daughter Keziah, to prevent an unsuitable marriage. An eagle outwits him by bringing Keziah's husband-to-be to the tower.

Animals often play important roles in the traditional stories of the Mayan people. Birds and beasts think and speak like humans, and occasionally take on human form. A rabbit—here called a coney—helps to free the imprisoned princess in the next tale.

Long ago, in the country we now call Guatemala, there lived a certain greedy king. His kingdom stretched from the mountains above Lake Atitlán to the edge of the jungle. In his storehouse were jars brimming with gold and jade, and with cocoa beans as prized as jewels. But his greatest treasure was his daughter, Princess Maix.

Maix was young and graceful. She was as slender as a reed that grew beside the lake and her hair was dyed the lavender-blue of the twilight sky. Many wealthy men wished to marry her.

"You will marry whoever offers the most

for you," declared the king.

"You cannot trade me like a monkey in the market!" cried Maix.

The king rubbed his hands. "I might exchange my one shy princess for a hundred bold warriors."

Maix shook her head. "I have already chosen my husband."

"Someone royal?" asked her father. "Someone rich?"

"Someone wonderful," the princess replied. "He is the man who plays the *chirimía* in the plaza, and his name is Tepe."

"That poor music-maker? The flute-blower? Never!" the king bellowed. "Your husband must be worthy of you—and worth much to me."

"Tck!" The princess clicked her tongue but dared say nothing more.

That night, before her father could pledge her to another, she slipped past the soldiers sleeping by her door and met the musician in the moonlit plaza. Without a sound, they fled into the shadows.

For three nights and three days, Maix and

Tepe trudged through the highlands, picking sweet green *injertos* from the trees to eat and resting at midday and midnight, for those were the unlucky times to travel. They left the cool mountains behind and plunged into the hot, steamy jungle. By day, bright-feathered macaws screeched in the trees and spider monkeys swung in the branches. By night, bats swooped overhead and scorpions scuttled underfoot. At last Maix and Tepe came to a village of strangers where people dressed in different clothes and spoke with different words.

"We have left your father's kingdom," said Tepe. "We are safe."

So that is where the princess and the poor man married. The village women gave Maix a cookpot and corn, and she learned to make the mash called *maadz*. The village men helped Tepe build a thatched hut. Every evening he sat by the door and played his *chirimía*, and the music was sweeter than any birdsong.

"These are riches enough for me," Maix declared.

Tepe shook his head. Soon the cookpot

would be empty. "I must find food for us," he told her. "Stay here, away from harm."

Alone, the music-maker went back to the hill country, keeping a sharp lookout for any of the king's warriors. Suddenly he stumbled on a clearing hidden behind a thicket of brambles. On one side was an orchard of plum trees whose branches bent with yellow fruit. On the other side was a large garden where corn grew tall, and sweet-potato vines twisted among the stalks. In the middle rose a huge house.

Tepe went to the door. "Greetings!" he called. "Is anyone at home?"

No one answered.

"You must be rich, whoever you are," Tepe said loudly. "One so rich will be glad to share with someone so poor as I."

Tepe gathered an armload of fruits and vegetables from the garden, and that night the princess's cookpot was full to the brim.

"Next time I'll go, too," Maix insisted. "We'll both fill sacks."

"It is dangerous . . ." Tepe began.

"No more for me than for you," the princess retorted.

A week later, when the sun was still a pale gold disc in the sky, Tepe and Maix visited the hidden garden together. Again, no one answered Tepe's call, and they fell to picking as fast as they could. Neither noticed the ground shake beneath their feet. Neither saw the shadow that suddenly darkened the rows. But both heard a voice rumbling louder than an exploding volcano, "GET OUT OF MY GARDEN!"

An ogre loomed over them. His head brushed the treetops and his legs were stouter than the thickest tree trunk. Two sharp teeth curled up like tusks from the corners of his mouth, and his hair was as bristly as a wild boar's.

"Thieves!" roared the ogre, snatching Tepe with one huge hand and Maix with the other.

"Let us go," Tepe pleaded. "We will never bother you again."

"*You* go." The ogre dropped Tepe. "I'll take the woman for my bride."

"She is a princess!" Tepe protested. "And she is my wife!"

"Not any longer." The ogre bound Maix with a stout rope and dragged her into his house.

Tepe ran back to the village. "Help me, neighbors!" he wailed. "A horrible ogre stole my wife!"

The villagers cowered in their huts and pretended not to understand him.

Then Tepe ran to the rock where the jaguar napped. "Help me, cousin cat," he called. "A horrible ogre stole my wife!"

Yawning, the jaguar said, "I will teach him a lesson."

It padded after Tepe to the ogre's house. But when that giant appeared in the doorway swinging a double-bladed battle-ax, the big cat trembled so hard, it shook off half its spots.

"Beg pardon," mumbled the jaguar, and dashed into the jungle.

Tepe went to the monkeys who hung by their tails in the mango trees. "Help me, little brothers. A horrible ogre stole my wife."

"Help a man?" they asked. "Men shoot arrows at us." They began throwing mangoes at Tepe.

Tepe visited the mouse's burrow. "A horrible ogre stole my wife. Please, friend mouse, gnaw the ropes that tie her."

"Free a WOMAN?" The mouse stared at him. "Women chase mice with brooms." With a squeak, it disappeared down the mousehole.

The music-maker trudged back to the ogre's garden. He held his head and moaned, "No one will help me rescue Maix."

"I will."

Tepe looked up and saw a rabbit chomping on a cucumber. "A coney?" Tepe shook his head. "You're not fierce like a jaguar or clever like a monkey. You don't even have sharp teeth like a mouse."

"But I have a plan," said the coney. "Come back at nightfall, and bring a shovel."

Help from a rabbit was better than no help at all. So when the evening star shone in the sky, the music-maker shouldered his shovel and returned to the garden.

"Dig," whispered Coney. "Make a tunnel beneath the ogre's corn, but don't wake the ogre!"

Maix had lulled the ogre to sleep with hot chocolate, and his snores were noisier than a howler monkey's shrieks. The princess watched Tepe from the doorway. He dug until dawn.

"The tunnel needs doors," said Coney. "Come back tonight."

That night, again the ogre slept. Again the princess watched and the music-maker dug. By sunup, the tunnel had twelve round door holes. "You're not yet finished," Coney told Tepe. "Tonight you must bring a machete."

Tepe retuned at twilight, a machete knife over his shoulder.

"Cut the brambles in the garden. Choose prickly bushes with the sharpest thorns," said Coney.

All night Tepe chopped briers with his machete. "Put the branches into the tunnel doorways," Coney ordered.

Gingerly, Tepe stuffed bristles into each

doorway. "I don't see how this saves Maix," he grumbled.

"Watch!" cried Coney.

The rabbit hopped to the house and pounded the wall with a huge hind foot. "Send out the princess!" he cried.

The ogre thundered out of the house. "You meddlesome, lop-eared, bobtailed trouble-maker!" he bellowed, lunging for the rabbit.

Coney jumped into a tunnel door hole. "Can't catch me!"

"Got you!" cried the ogre, and thrust his arm into the hole. But he did not feel a velvety rabbit skin. Instead he caught hold of a prickly bramble. "Yi!" he yelped.

"Over here!" Coney called from a different door.

"I see you!" roared the ogre. But as soon as he stuck his head in the tunnel, a thorny branch poked his eye.

Wild with anger, the ogre scrambled from hole to hole, grabbing for the rabbit. But Coney was always a jump ahead, twitching his nose and wriggling his ears. The brambles did not even ruffle the rabbit's fur, but they ripped the ogre's clothes and scratched and scraped him from foot to face. As the ogre bent over the twelfth hole, the music-maker swung his machete and shouted, "This is for the princess!"

The big knife whistled so close to the ogre's scalp that it shaved off every hair. The ogre rubbed his bald head and groaned. Soon everyone would know that a little coney had fooled him. With a howl of humiliation, the ogre fled over the hills and disappeared into the jungle.

Tepe hurried to Maix and cut the ropes that bound her. "At last!" said the princess. "It's past time for our supper."

The rabbit was already having supper in the ogre's garden. Maix and Tepe bid him farewell and hurried back to the village.

Everyone celebrated their safe return. Women danced with copper bells, men beat the two-toned drums, and children blew clay whistles. But the most joyful sounds were the notes played on the *chirimía* by the music-maker for Princess Maix.

Psyche

The Greeks first told the myth of "Psyche" more than two thousand years ago. But Psyche isn't just a princess from the past. She belongs to the present, too, for many favorite fairy tales borrow bits and pieces from her story.

Both the French "Beauty and the Beast" and the Norwegian "East of the Sun and West of the Moon" use the idea of a beastly bridegroom. Similar tales are found in Sicily, India, Russia, and Mongolia.

The French and German Cinderellas, as well as Umusha Mwaice, a Cinderella from the Congo, share jealous sisters with Psyche. The envious queen in "Snow White" echoes the Greek Goddess of Beauty—Aphrodite. Bad-tempered stepmothers in Italian, Korean, Russian, and Vietnamese Cinderella stories also imitate her by assigning impossible tasks.

Psyche's peeking into a forbidden box is copied by curious maidens in European and

Asian fairy tales who open secret doors and pry into cupboards and trunks.

Eros, the Greek God of Love, is familiar, too. Psyche's tall and handsome bridegroom has become Cupid, the curly-haired cherub on Valentine cards.

A sip of ambrosia from the cup of the gods makes Psyche immortal. But it is the story about this long-ago Greek princess that is truly everlasting.

Once upon a time, so the mythmakers said, there lived a Greek king who had three daughters. The oldest princess was very pretty. The second princess was quite charming. The youngest princess, whose name was Psyche, was so lovely that even the flowers turned their heads to look at her.

Praise for Psyche's beauty spread throughout Greece and soon reached the ears of the gods and goddesses who dwelled high on Mount

Olympus.

"Ridiculous!" scoffed the goddess Aphrodite. "This princess is only a girl. *I* am the Goddess of Beauty."

Aphrodite pushed aside the curtain of clouds and inspected the earth below. No people worshipped in the temples built to honor her. No scented smoke curled up from the altars.

"Psyche is to blame!" The goddess clenched her teeth. "But she shall pay for stealing my glory."

Day by day, as Psyche became lovelier, her friends became fewer. Other maidens, even her own sisters, were jealous of her. Men, dazzled by her beauty, were afraid to speak to her.

"I wish I had snakes for hair and snaggle-teeth," the princess declared. "Then someone might love me."

Dismayed by her words, the king asked the all-knowing Oracle of Delphi what match might be in store for his youngest daughter.

"Psyche's husband awaits her on Mount Olympus. But," the old priestess warned, "he will not be human."

The king raged and the queen wept, knowing full well the perils on that mountain. Only Psyche was calm. "If that is what's foretold," she said, "then so it must be."

The next day, Psyche climbed Mount Olympus. Halfway up, she stopped to rest, pillowing her head on her arms. Would it be her fate to wed some savage beast, a bear or wolf? Perhaps a terrible winged serpent would swoop down from the darkening sky. Shivering, the princess wrapped herself in her cloak and closed her eyes.

When Aphrodite looked down and saw Psyche alone on the mountainside, she sent at once for her son, Eros.

"How quickly you came," Aphrodite said, smiling at the handsome winged God of Love. "You are as swift as an eagle."

Eros shrugged.

"Yet one of your arrows flies faster still, and never misses its target."

Eros nodded, wondering why his mother had summoned him.

"If only I had such skills!" The goddess stroked her son's feathered wings. "I count on you to help me. Wound a prideful Greek princess with one of your arrows . . ."

Alarmed, Eros jumped back. "I would not harm anyone, not even for you," he replied. "A sting from my arrow causes lovesickness, nothing more."

"But that's enough!" cried Aphrodite. "I *want* this girl to fall in love. I want her to love the worst, the ugliest, the most horrible creature in the whole world."

Eros eyed his beautiful mother. Her ill humor, like storm clouds, would soon blow over. "Let me think on it," he said.

"It must be now," Aphrodite insisted, "while the princess slumbers on the slopes of Mount Olympus. Strike her now!"

Eros had to obey. Aphrodite was a powerful goddess as well as his mother. He plunged the tip of an arrow into the nectar of love, sweet and sticky as honey, and flew in search of the princess.

Aphrodite was pleased with her scheme. Eros would prick Psyche with a love-soaked arrow. Then, when that unlucky princess chanced to wake, her lovesick gaze would fall upon some hideous monster. Aphrodite herself would see to that.

But things did not go as the Goddess of Beauty had planned. As soon as Eros set eyes on Psyche, asleep in the moonlight, his heart began to pound. He had never seen so beautiful a maiden. His hand shook as he picked up his arrow, and it slipped through his fingers. Instead of piercing Psyche's heart, the arrow scraped his own knuckle.

"Clumsy!" Eros licked off the trickle of blood.

But it was too late. The winged god was already helplessly, hopelessly in love with Psyche. Gazing at her, he knew he must protect her from Aphrodite's fury. Gently, Eros lifted the sleeping princess and bore her to his palace.

When Psyche awoke, she rubbed her eyes in astonishment. She wasn't on Mount Olympus, nor had she been dragged to the den of a wild beast. She was in the garden of a magnificent palace. Fountains splashed into pools beneath trees laden with fruit. Except for birdsongs, she neither saw nor heard anything until a voice said, "Welcome, Princess. Everything here is yours."

Within the marble palace, she found a table laid with a supper of meats and cheeses and sweets of every kind. As she ate, she listened to the music of a lyre. But she did not see the hand that played it, nor any human form at all.

Psyche slept that night on a couch of softest goose down. She drifted from dream to dream until a sudden rush of wings awakened her. Something stood by her couch, concealed by darkness.

"Who is there?" gasped the princess.

"One who loves you," a voice answered.

Psyche found his words sweet and his voice kind. She talked with the mysterious visitor throughout the night. But when the morning star faded, he left as suddenly as he had come.

The days that followed were delightful for the princess. Unseen hands did her every bidding,

and she wanted for nothing. When night fell, a beating of wings announced her visitor. Until dawn, he entertained her with stories and enchanted her with songs. Yet shadows always hid her suitor's face, and whenever she asked his name, he answered only, "One who loves you."

One night Psyche said, "I miss my family. I wish my sisters could pay a visit."

"That would not be wise."

"Please," she begged. "My father deserves news of me."

His wings rustled sharply as if whipped by a sudden gust of wind. "Very well," he agreed, and asked Zephyr the West Wind to carry Psyche's sisters to the palace.

Psyche greeted her sisters joyfully. They looked about in wonder and stared at her many treasures.

"Who has given you all this?" the older sister asked.

"I cannot say," Psyche confessed. "He disappears at dawn."

"Don't you even know what he looks like?" asked the younger.

"I have felt the curls upon his head . . ."

"A sheep has curly hair."

"And he has strong wings with soft feathers . . ."

"Then he is not a man!" cried one sister. "He is a monster! That's what the oracle foretold."

"He might be feeding you now . . . fattening you first . . . to DEVOUR YOU!" added the other.

"But . . ." Psyche bit her tongue. Perhaps he did use darkness to hide something dreadful. "But . . . what can I do?"

"Without his knowing, light a lamp," the sisters suggested. "See for yourself what sort of a creature he is."

After Zephyr had sped her sisters away, the princess hid a small oil lamp beneath the couch. But she could not conceal her guilt so easily.

Her visitor noticed Psyche's distress. "You are upset," he said. "I shall not stay."

"Don't go!" cried Psyche. "Rest first—on the couch."

"If that is what you wish," he agreed. Yawning, he lay down and closed his eyes.

When she knew by his breathing that he had fallen asleep, Psyche lighted the lamp and held it over his head. Its beam shone upon the fairest youth that the princess had ever seen.

"Can it be . . . Eros? Are you . . . you *are* the God of Love!"

Psyche's hand trembled, and the lamp tipped. Smoking oil spattered on the god's wing and ran down his shoulder.

Eros cried out in pain. He saw Psyche bending over him, still grasping the lamp. With scorched wing dangling, he vanished into the night sky.

For many weeks, the princess wept and waited. When the god did not return, she vowed, "I will search for him, though it take me all my life."

Psyche wandered through the valleys and

woodlands of Greece, calling for Eros. On a hilltop, she came to a deserted temple honoring Aphrodite. She bent down before the altar.

"Hear me, O goddess. Help me to find your son."

Aphrodite heard Psyche's plea. "How dare you ask for *my* help," she shrieked, "when Eros is lying burned and bandaged?"

"By your leave, I might prove my love for him," said Psyche.

"Prove yourself to me first!"

The goddess seized great baskets of barley and millet and poppy seeds, brought to the temple long before as offerings. She scattered them everywhere. "Separate these grains by nightfall."

Left alone, the princess stared at the seeds. No one could do such an enormous task. Then she noticed a long line of ants marching into the temple.

"Pity me," she told them, "for my task is hopeless."

As if obeying a hidden command, tens of thousands of ants swarmed across the stone floor. Picking up the tiny seeds, they swiftly, silently, carried the grains to their proper baskets.

When Aphrodite returned, she found everything in order. "Trickery's afoot!" she muttered.

The goddess threw Psyche a crust of bread for her supper and bid her sleep on the cold floor. In the morning, she smiled to see the princess with red-rimmed eyes circled with shadows.

"In the thicket by the stream are sheep with golden fleece," said Aphrodite. "Fetch a bundle of their wool."

Psyche had to shade her eyes to look at the sheep, for their coats gleamed as brightly as the sun. But she saw no playful lambs or gentle ewes among the flock. All were fierce rams, with sharp horns and wicked hoofs. "Such dreadful beasts!" she cried. "How can I shear them?"

The reeds beside the stream began to quiver. From their midst a voice murmured, "When the sheep come here to drink, hasten to the thicket. Pluck the wool that clings to the bushes."

Psyche did not know who had spoken. Was it a river god or just the wind in the rushes? But she did as she was told and safely gathered an armload of the golden fleece to carry back to Aphrodite.

The goddess snatched the wool. "Worse luck the next time, you wretched girl," she snapped. "Know you of the underworld?"

The princess nodded. She had heard of its terrors.

"Go there. Tell the goddess Persephone that I am worn from tending my sick son and need some of her beauty magic."

Psyche knew that no tiny ants, no voice from the reeds could aid her on this dangerous journey. Yet as she stumbled past an old tower, a voice called from within.

"Look for a coin and a cake in yonder cave. Give the coin to the ferryman. Feed the cake to the three-headed watchdog."

The princess obeyed, too frightened to do otherwise. In exchange for the coin, the ferryman rowed her across the River Styx to the dark and dreary underworld. While the monstrous dog that guarded the entrance gobbled the cake, Psyche slipped into Persephone's palace.

The goddess, hearing the reason for her errand, gave her a small box. "Take this to Aphrodite. But take care! Powerful magic is inside."

Psyche returned quickly, relieved to leave the underworld behind. As she drew close to Aphrodite's temple, she hesitated, staring at the box in her hand. Did she not need a bit of beauty, too, to look lovely for Eros? Cautiously, Psyche lifted the lid of the box. A sweet-smelling mist swirled up.

"Oh!" Psyche fell to the path.

There the God of Love found her overcome by a deadly sleep. He wiped the clinging vapor from her eyes, returned it to the box, and awakened Psyche with a touch from one of his arrows.

"You have come back!" cried the princess.

"I have never left you," Eros replied.

Then Psyche knew that he had sent the ants. His voice had spoken from the reeds and called from the tower. She held out her arms. "Stay with me now."

"First you must take the box to Aphrodite. And I, too, must attend to something."

While the princess hurried back to Aphrodite's temple, Eros flew to the heights of Mount Olympus. There he told Zeus, ruler of all the gods, of Psyche's many trials. Zeus sent a messenger to bring both the princess and the Goddess of Beauty to him.

"Psyche has proved herself worthy," Zeus decreed. He handed her a cup of ambrosia. "This is the nectar of the gods. Drink it and live among us always."

Aphrodite watched, speechless with anger, as Psyche sipped from the cup of immortality. But her good humor returned when Eros reminded her that if the princess was in the heavens, Psyche could not turn heads on earth. The temples to the Goddess of Beauty would no longer be neglected.

◆ ◆ ◆

Then, before all the gods and goddesses gathered on Mount Olympus, the princess and the God of Love were wed. Psyche and Eros lived happily together forever . . . and ever.

Notes on the Stories

The Moon Maidens

According to old Chinese beliefs, the sun, the moon, the wind, and the water were all ruled by particular spirits or dieties. The moon spirit was *yin*, or female, while the sun god was masculine. In this unusual legend, "The Moon Maidens," those roles are reversed. It is based upon a version from Frances Carpenter's *Tales of a Chinese Grandmother* (Rutland, Vt.: Charles E. Tuttle Co., 1973).

Gulnara

"Gulnara," a tale from *The Arabian Nights*, isn't often told, yet it seems familiar. A baby cast adrift is a common theme in a number of Mediterranean and Asian cultures. Most famous is the prophet Moses, who was rescued as an infant from his cradle in the bullrushes. Another legendary figure is Prince Rhya Kong of Siam (now

Thailand), whose royal father sent him downstream in a golden bowl. This adaptation draws on James Riordan's "Gulnara, the Brave and Clever Maiden," *Tales of the Arabian Nights* (New York: Rand McNally and Co., 1985).

Prince Ivan and the Frog Princess

Story collector A. N. Afanasyev has been labeled "The Russian Grimm" for his devotion to preserving ethnic folklore. The idea of a spellbound princess disguised in a frog skin is well-known in Slavic cultures. This Russian version is notable for including that tricky, good-bad witch, Baba-Yaga. A. N. Afanasyev, "The Frog Princess," *Russian Folktales* (New York: Random House, 1980).

Two Brides for Five Heads

The source for this South African tale is "The Story of Five Heads" in *Folktales of All Nations*, a comprehensive collection of world folklore by F. H. Lee (New York: Tudor Publishing Co., 1930). Of considerable help in specific background of Xhosa customs and beliefs was Aubrey Elliot's *The Magic World of the Xhosa* (New York: Charles Scribner's Sons, 1970).

King Thrushbeard

Brothers Jacob and Wilhelm Grimm, scholars and teachers, are best remembered as folklorists. In 1812, they published the first volume of *Kinderund Hausmärchen,* or *Children's and Household Tales*, and the second volume appeared two years later. Now these two-hundred-plus stories have been reprinted in seventy languages. This adaptation most closely follows the version in *Grimms' Fairy Tales* (New York: Grosset and Dunlap Inc., 1945).

The Princess and the Music-Maker

"The Princess and the Music-Maker" is an adaptation of an oral tale, "The Daughter of a King Who Was Carried Away by a Poor Person," from the Lake Atitlán region of Guatemala. It was recorded and translated by anthropologist James Sexton for his book *Mayan Folktales* (New York: Anchor Books, 1992).

105

Psyche

The story of Psyche, the immortal Greek
princess, was a familiar allegory in the
ancient world. The Romans made this
legend a part of their own mythology,
and Apuleius, a Latin writer, recorded it
in the second century. This retelling relies
on Thomas Bullfinch's *The Age of Fable*
(New York: International Collector's
Library, 1968).